Contents

For Clare

First published in 1987 by
The Hamlyn Publishing Group Limited
Bridge House, 69 London Road, Twickenham, Middlesex TW1 3SB
Copyright © The Hamlyn Publishing Group Limited 1987

ISBN 0 600 55420 1

Printed in Hong Kong by Mandarin Offset

Little Bear Tales

Written and illustrated by Gillian Chapman

HAMLYN

The Fancy Dress Party

Little Bear was getting very excited as it would soon be his birthday. He made a list of all the friends he wanted to come to his party. He carefully wrote out the invitation cards in his best handwriting and posted them through his friends' letter boxes.

Little Bear's party was going to be extra special this year — it was going to be a fancy dress party.

Little Bear started to think about his own fancy dress costume. He searched in the cupboard and found a box of odd scraps of paper, string, card and bits that he had thought might come in handy one day. "I wonder what I could make out of these?" he thought. "I want my costume to be the best *and* the most unusual!"

The days passed by, and the Party Day grew nearer.
Little Bear couldn't think what he should wear. He
racked his brains!
   Well, he did have a lot of ideas . . . a robot bear
. . . a dragon . . . a banana . . . even Mickey Mouse!
But he didn't like any of these. He wanted to dress up
as something **very** different — it was his party after
all and he wanted to surprise all his friends!

8

His Mum was busy with all the party cooking. "Mum, what can I go as?" sighed Little Bear. "Oh, I don't know," said Mum crossly. "Stop worrying me. I've a lot to do. I'm trying to get everything ready for your party tomorrow. Go and have a look through your picture books — you might get some ideas there."

The Big Day arrived. The postman brought lots of cards. Little Bear was so excited. Mum and Dad had bought him a lovely new blue scooter. Little Bear was thrilled! Little Brother gave him some rather sticky

To L.B. xx

sweets which he had bought himself. (He had eaten some, but Little Bear was too happy to notice.)

Grandpa had sent a big parcel. When Little Bear opened it, he found a lovely book full of colour photographs of places and people from different parts of the world.

The World

All the family started getting things ready for the party. Mum laid the table with all the tasty food while Dad decorated the room with streamers and lots of balloons. Little Brother couldn't wait to get into his costume — he was a Maharajah with a grand moustache! But where was Little Bear? He was supposed to be helping. He'd locked himself in his bedroom!

All Little Bear's friends arrived in their fancy dress costumes — there was a clown, a pirate, a flower and a fairy. They had all brought presents for Little Bear — but where was he? If he didn't hurry, they would start the tea without him. It looked so delicious they could hardly wait.
Hurry up Little Bear!

Then the door burst open and there was Little Bear! What a big surprise! Little Bear was dressed up as . . . the Statue of Liberty! Who would have guessed? Where did he get the idea? Why, perhaps it was from Grandpa's book!

A Day at the Seaside

It was another hot day at the seaside and Little Bear was thinking of ways to cool off. He was already wearing his snazzy swimming trunks — but it was so very hot! At last he decided to go and paddle in the sea. Grandpa was watching from his deckchair just to make sure no harm came to him.

Little Bear tried to splash Grandpa with the water—
but he was much too far away!

After a while, Little Bear became bored with all the
splashing, and decided to go and treat himself to an
ice lolly with some of his pocket money. As he was
walking back, licking his lolly, he passed the boating
lake. "Yes, I've enough money left. I'll go and find
Little Brother and take him for a row!"

15

Little Bear rushed back to where the family were sunbathing on the beach. Excitedly, Little Bear told Little Brother about the boats. At first Little Brother was rather nervous at the idea. But after Little Bear promised to look after him and not let him get wet, off they went to the boating lake together. There was a nice little yellow boat! Just the thing. So they paddled away, and soon Little Brother was enjoying himself as much as Little Bear.

Little Bear was dreaming that he was the captain of a ship and Little Brother was the crew. They were sailing on the high seas and there were sharks all around . . . A shout shattered his dream. It was the boatman calling, "Come along! Your time is up!" So they slowly paddled their way back to the shore.

But when they got back to the beach, oh dear, Grandpa was nowhere to be found! Everyone began to look for him. The bears ran up and down the sand calling, "Grandpa! Grandpa!" very loudly.

They looked everywhere! They looked on the pier, and in the amusement arcade, even behind the candy floss stall . . .!

18

They looked in the Punch-and-Judy tent. They asked the deckchair man and the boy selling rock, "Have you seen Grandpa?" Where could he be?

Now the bears were getting tired, and they had nowhere else to look!

Then they saw a deckchair, covered in newspaper. The paper was gently moving up and down. Puzzled, the bears forgot the search for Grandpa and went to investigate.

Closer and closer they crept. Not only was the paper moving up and down, but strange whistling noises were coming from underneath!

"What can this be?" While they spoke to each other in low whispers the newspaper gave one mighty roar . . .
. . . the bears fell backwards in surprise, then all at once the

newspaper floated away. And what do
you think? There was Grandpa,
fast asleep underneath!
  The bears laughed and laughed as Grandpa awoke
with a jump! But how very pleased they were to have
found their most favourite friend!

The Attic

It was a wet winter's afternoon and Little Bear was bored, so Dad suggested that they tidy up the attic.

Little Bear and Tibby the cat had never been up into the attic before, and they were quite excited. Dad got the ladder from the shed and climbed up through the hatch. It was very dark before Dad turned the light on, and very, very dusty as no one had been in the attic for a long time.

There were so many boxes, suitcases, old carpets and lampshades! Things that everyone had forgotten. There were also lots of cobwebs. At one end of the attic there was a large box, full of blankets and curtains, but one look inside told them that it would take a long time to sort out, so they started their tidying up at the other end of the attic.

Tibby, however, did not care for cobwebs.

"Oh, look what I've found!" said Little Bear. There were some very old Christmas tree decorations in a box and lots of old Christmas cards. "Perhaps we could cut out the pictures on the cards and make gift tags and calendars." Then Little Bear found some old toys and piles of comics. So he sat down on a battered hat box and started to read them.

"Come on," said Dad, "no time for you to read them now. We'll dust them off and take them downstairs to read later." Dad was using the hose brush on the vacuum cleaner to suck up the dust in the beams. He had his overalls on and Little Bear had his old clothes on too, which was just as well as he was starting to look very grubby! There was so much dust about — it was everywhere!

"I wonder what's inside this trunk?" said Dad, wiping the dust off the lid. He heaved open the heavy lid and they saw it was full of old photograph albums. "Goodness me – I'd forgotten we had these," said Dad. "Let's sit down and have a look through some of them." So they both sat down on the lid of the trunk and started to look through the photographs. Dad pointed out who was who, as Little Bear didn't recognize everyone.

In the albums there were lots of photographs of Little Bear and Little Brother as young cubs. There were pictures of the bears on holiday and at parties.

Some were very funny — like the one of Auntie wearing her best hat and a very blurred photograph of Grandpa taking apples from next door's garden when he thought no-one was watching!

Little Bear thought that was a very good joke.

Then they heard a voice from downstairs — it was Mum wondering what all the laughter was about. Dad and Little Bear had forgotten the time! Mum was calling them to come down and have their dinner. They packed away the old photographs, and were just about to go back down the ladder when they remembered Tibby the cat. Where was she? Perhaps she was already downstairs — but no, Mum hadn't seen her. So they started to look around the boxes and bundles in the attic calling, "Tibby, Tibby . . ."

Then a very faint "Me-ow" was heard coming from the big box — the one with all the old curtains and blankets. Sure enough, there was Tibby stretched out enjoying the warmth.

She had whiled away the afternoon asleep in the box and hadn't noticed the time passing either!